P9-DWP-933

Nia
the Night Owl
Fairy

Special thanks to Narinder Dhami

If you purchased this book without a cover, you should be aware that this book is stolen property. It was reported as "unsold and destroyed" to the publisher, and neither the author nor the publisher has received any payment for this "stripped book."

No part of this work may be reproduced, stored in a retrieval system, or transmitted in any form or by any means, electronic, mechanical, photocopying, recording, or otherwise, without written permission of the publisher. For information regarding permission, write to Rainbow Magic Limited c/o HIT Entertainment, 830 South Greenville Avenue, Allen, TX 75002-3320.

ISBN 978-0-545-27048-9

Copyright © 2010 by Rainbow Magic Limited.

Previously published as Twilight Fairies #5: *Yasmin the Night Owl Fairy* by Orchard U.K. in 2010.

All rights reserved. Published by Scholastic Inc., 557 Broadway, New York, NY 10012, by arrangement with Rainbow Magic Limited.

SCHOLASTIC and associated logos are trademarks and/or registered trademarks of Scholastic Inc. RAINBOW MAGIC is a trademark of Rainbow Magic Limited. Reg. U.S. Patent & Trademark Office and other countries. HIT and the HIT logo are trademarks of HIT Entertainment Limited.

12 11 10 9 8 7 6 5 4 3 2 1   11 12 13 14 15/0

Printed in the U.S.A.   40

First Scholastic Printing, July 2011

Nia
the Night Owl
Fairy

by Daisy Meadows

SCHOLASTIC INC.

New York   Toronto   London   Auckland
Sydney   Mexico City   New Delhi   Hong Kong

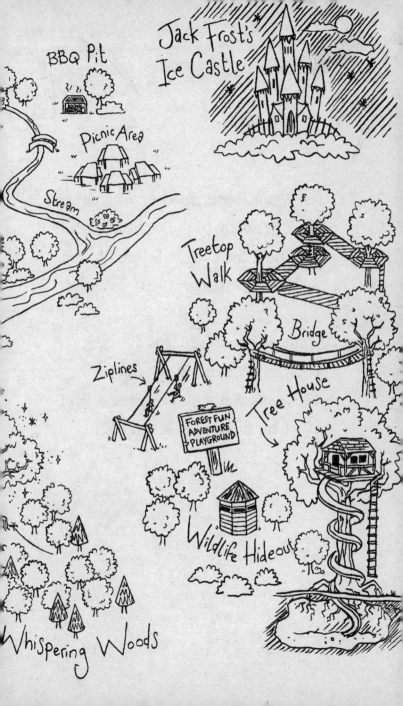

The Night Fairies' special magic powers
Bring harmony to the nighttime hours.
But now their magic belongs to me,
And I'll cause chaos, you shall see!

In sunset, moonlight, and starlight, too,
There'll be no more sweet dreams for you.
From evening dusk to morning light,
I am the master of the night!

Contents

Night or Day?   1

Magic Owl   15

Snoring Goblins   25

Topsy-Turvy   35

Zipline Show!   49

Shadow Swoops In   59

Night or Day?

"Hold on tight, Kirsty," Rachel called to her best friend, Kirsty Tate. "We're almost there!"

"I'm right behind you, Rachel!" Kirsty called back.

The girls were walking carefully across the wobbly bridge in the Forest Fun Adventure Playground. The wooden bridge was part of a high-ropes course. It was strung between two trees way above the ground. It swayed and wobbled gently as the girls moved across it, making them shriek with laughter.

"Oh, this is too much fun!" Kirsty gasped. "I love Camp Stargaze, Rachel. There's so much to do here."

The girls and their parents were spending a week of summer vacation at Camp Stargaze, and the Forest Fun playground was in a clearing in the woods on the edge of the campground. There was a treetop walk, a few hideouts, and two ziplines next to each other, as well as the wobbly bridge. The biggest tree in the clearing, the one the girls were heading toward on the wobbly bridge, had a wooden treehouse in its branches.

There was also a twisty slide that
wrapped around the tree's trunk and led
all the way down to an
underground fort built
below the roots of
the tree. It was late
afternoon, just
after snack time,
and the girls were
still enjoying the
warmth of the
summer sun.

"I know," Rachel agreed. "Camp
Stargaze is amazing. And not only that,
we're in the middle of another exciting
fairy adventure, too!"

Shortly after Rachel and Kirsty had
arrived at the camp, their fairy friends
had asked for their help once again.

The girls soon met the Night Fairies, who were responsible for making sure that the hours between dusk and dawn were peaceful in both the human and fairy worlds. They did this work with the help of their special bags of magic fairy dust. But while the Night Fairies were at a party under the stars, Jack Frost and his goblins had stolen the magic bags from them! Jack Frost was determined to cause nighttime chaos. With his icy magic, he sent the goblins to hide the bags in the human world. But Rachel, Kirsty, and the Night Fairies had already found four of the seven bags, and they were hoping to find the others, too.

"Rachel, Kirsty!" a voice shouted. "We're over here."

The girls glanced up and saw their new

friends Matt and Lucas hanging out of one of the treehouse windows. Rachel

and Kirsty wobbled to the end of the bridge and went to join them inside the big treehouse. "Have you been on the ziplines yet?" Lucas asked with a grin.

Kirsty shook her head. "I think I need to recover from the wobbly bridge first!" she replied.

Matt was still hanging out of the window. "Look, Lucas," he said, pointing down at the ground below them. "There's your mom and Lizzy."

Lucas's mom and his little sister were wandering through the clearing. They

waved up at the treehouse, and Lucas, Rachel, Kirsty, and Matt waved back.

"Let's go down the twisty slide and say hi!" Rachel suggested.

The top of the silver slide was just outside the treehouse door. Rachel climbed onto it and then immediately shot down with a shriek of surprise.

"It's really slippery!" she cried as she disappeared from view.

"Watch out, Rachel!" Kirsty yelled as she jumped on the slide, too. "Here I come!"

Laughing, Rachel zoomed around the trunk of the tree, then through the

trapdoor to the underground fort at the bottom. She tumbled off the end of the slide and onto a soft cushion. Kirsty came flying into the underground house a few seconds later, and the two girls grinned at each other.

"Here come the boys!" Rachel said as they heard Matt and Lucas sliding toward them.

First Matt, and then Lucas, tumbled into the underground fort. Next, all four of them climbed out and ran to join Lucas's mom and Lizzy. They were staring very closely at a large, leafy bush.

"What are you looking at?" Lucas asked curiously.

"Porcupines," Lucas's mom replied. Both her and Lizzy's eyes were wide with delight. "Look!"

Rachel and Kirsty peeked into the bush, and saw two small porcupines scampering around in the leaves.

"Aren't they cute?" said Rachel as the porcupines scurried back and forth. Just then, Kirsty heard a rustling noise in the undergrowth behind them. She spun around and caught a glimpse of gray fur and a black-and-white striped head. Quickly, she nudged Rachel.

"There's a badger over there!" Kirsty whispered.

Rachel, Lucas, and the others watched

in amazement as the
badger came into
view. He was
sniffing through
the leaves in
search of something
to eat.

"This is great!" Matt
said, looking excited as the
badger hurried past, not even noticing
them. "I've never seen a badger *or* a
porcupine during the day before."

Kirsty frowned. "Matt's right," she said
to Rachel. "Don't porcupines and badgers
usually come out at night?"

"Let's go up to the wildlife hideout in
the treetops and look for more animals,"
Rachel suggested. The hideout was a
special shelter where people could watch

animals without scaring them away.

"We're going back to camp to play football," Lucas told the girls. "See you later."

The wildlife hideout was hidden behind

a canopy of leaves in the branches of one of the trees. Kirsty and Rachel climbed the ladder and then hurried along one of the wooden walkways that connected the treetop trail. When they arrived, the hideout was empty. There were wildlife posters on the walls. Two pairs of binoculars lay on the seat in front of the window.

"Look, Rachel, we can see the camp,"

Kirsty pointed out, picking up a pair of
the binoculars.

"And past the camp, too," Rachel
added. She took the other binoculars
and looked through them. "We can see
the river we sailed up to get to the camp.
And I can see cows and sheep in the field
across the river — OH!" Rachel looked
startled.

"What is it?" Kirsty asked.

"The farm animals are all fast asleep!" Rachel told her. "Isn't that strange?"

Kirsty focused her binoculars on the field across the river. Now she could also see that the cows and sheep were all sleeping happily!

"But it's still daytime!" Kirsty pointed out, confused. "Why are the nighttime creatures like the badger and porcupines awake during the day? And why are the animals like cows and sheep, who *should* be awake, sound asleep?"

Magic Owl

"Do you think this could have something to do with Jack Frost stealing the Night Fairies' magic dust?" Rachel suggested, looking worried.

"It must!" Kirsty insisted with a frown. "After all, everything's been going wrong at nighttime since Jack Frost and his goblins stole the magic bags."

"But it *isn't* nighttime," Rachel said. "The sun's still shining. It's not even dusk yet!"

The girls exchanged confused glances. Suddenly a soft, hooting sound outside the wildlife hideout made them both almost jump out of their skin.

"What's that noise?" Kirsty cried nervously.

"I think it might be an owl," Rachel suggested. "And it sounds like it's close by. Let's go and take a look."

The girls crept away from the hideout. They could still hear the gentle *whoo-whoo* sound, and they followed it, walking along one of the wooden bridges toward the treehouse. Suddenly, Kirsty clutched Rachel's arm.

"Look!" she whispered, "There, on

that big branch near the roof of the treehouse!"

Rachel looked where Kirsty was pointing and her face lit up with delight. A nest had been built in the crook of the branch, and inside it sat a brown owl, hooting softly. Three fluffy baby owls with large round eyes were cuddled up next to her.

"Oh, aren't they cute?" Rachel whispered to Kirsty as the mother and baby owls all blinked their big eyes at them. They didn't seem nervous, but the girls were careful to speak quietly and not startle them in any way. "But shouldn't *they* be asleep, too?"

"Yes, they should," Kirsty agreed. "Owls are only supposed to be awake at night."

Suddenly the girls heard the flapping of wings overhead. They glanced up and saw a snow-white owl, its feathers beautifully streaked with silver, hovering just above the roof of the treehouse. As Kirsty looked a little closer, she saw that the owl's feathers were sparkling and glittering in the bright sunlight.

"Rachel, I think that's fairy magic!" Kirsty gasped, breathless with excitement as she pointed out the dazzling feathers.

"Are you a *magic* owl?" Rachel asked.

The snowy owl hooted softly and flapped her wings.

"I think she wants us to go with her!" Kirsty exclaimed.

Immediately, the owl flew off the treehouse roof and circled above the girls. She shook her wings and a cloud of rainbow-colored sparkles floated downward, showering Rachel and Kirsty with fairy magic.

"We're becoming fairies, Kirsty!" Rachel laughed as she felt herself quickly shrinking down.

The mother and baby owls watched in astonishment as the girls turned into tiny fairies with shimmering wings on their backs. Then the snow-white owl shook her own wings again. Rachel and Kirsty both shut their eyes as they were whirled away in a burst of magic fairy dust. Rachel's heart thumped with excitement. She wondered where the owl was taking them!

A few seconds later, the girls opened their eyes to find themselves flying alongside the snowy owl over the familiar

sights of Fairyland. They could see the
royal palace with its four pink towers
and the fairies' red-and-white toadstool
houses. But as they swooped down,
Rachel could tell that something wasn't
quite right.

"Isn't this strange,
Kirsty?" she
called. "It's
so *quiet*."

"I know," Kirsty
replied with a frown.

"Oh!" Rachel exclaimed suddenly as
they flew lower. "Now I can see why,
Kirsty. All the fairies are fast asleep!"

Kirsty realized that Rachel was right.
Everywhere the girls looked, they could
see sleeping fairies. Some were lying in
the meadow by the river among the grass

and wildflowers. Others were stretched
out on the Fairyland beach in the
sunshine. As Rachel and Kirsty flew past
the toadstool houses, they peeked into the
windows and saw fairies asleep in beds
and in chairs. One had even fallen asleep
while baking a cake in the kitchen!

There were lots of fairies in
the palace gardens, too. Even
the Night Fairies were lying
among the flowers, dozing
peacefully. One of them
was sleeping upright,
leaning against the
trunk of a tree.

"This is all because
of Jack Frost!"
Kirsty sighed.

"Do you think we should wake the fairies up?"

"Let's see what the magic owl wants us to do," Rachel suggested.

The owl was just ahead of the girls. She was hovering in midair, checking to make sure they were still following her. Rachel and Kirsty rushed to catch up, and the owl led them to a tall tree in the middle of the palace gardens. There, nestled at the foot of a tree, the girls saw a fairy. She was fast asleep, just like the others. "It's Nia the Night Owl Fairy!" Kirsty whispered to Rachel.

Snoring Goblins

The girls watched as the magic owl hooted gently. She flapped her wings and stared anxiously at Nia. But Nia didn't even stir. The owl began to hoot more loudly, batting her wings up and down.

Whoo! Whoo! Whoo!

Suddenly, Nia moved her head slightly.

Rachel and Kirsty watched with relief as
the fairy's eyes gradually flickered open
and she yawned, wiggling her wings.

"Hello, Nia," Rachel said with a smile.
Nia's eyes now opened
wide and she sat up.
She wore a pink-
and-white spotted
T-shirt with a
picture of an owl
on it, cutoff
jeans over leggings,
and sparkly pink sneakers.

"Oh, Rachel and Kirsty, it's you!" Nia
exclaimed in surprise, tossing back her
long dark hair. "I'm so happy to see you.
How did you get here?"

"A magic owl brought us!" Kirsty
laughed, and the snowy owl hooted in

agreement. Nia noticed the owl for the first time, and her face lit up.

"Shadow, you're *such* a smart bird!" Nia declared, glancing around the palace gardens at all the other sleeping fairies. "Girls, this is Shadow, a magic owl who lives in Fairyland. She obviously realized that something was very wrong here, and went to find you."

"Something's very wrong in the human world, too, Nia," Rachel explained. "All the nighttime animals are awake during the day, and all the daytime animals are asleep."

"And now all the fairies are asleep, too!" Kirsty added.

Nia shook her head in dismay. "This is all because my bag of magic sleep dust is missing." She sighed. "That's why everyone's sleep is all mixed up! Girls, will you help me get my bag back from those troublesome goblins?"

"Of course we will," Rachel said. Kirsty nodded in agreement, and Shadow the magic owl looked pleased and hooted with satisfaction.

"Then let's return to Camp Stargaze right away!" Nia cried. And with one flick of her wrist, a stream of shimmering sparkles whirled from her wand and surrounded them all, including Shadow.

A few seconds later they were all back

in the Forest Fun Adventure Playground on the edge of the campsite. Luckily, nobody else was around. Rachel and Kirsty were still fairy-size, but Shadow had changed back to the size of an ordinary owl. She flew up into one of the trees and settled on a branch.

"Now, where are those goblins?" Nia wondered. "I can sense that they're around here somewhere with my bag of sleep dust."

The three friends began to search the playground. But as they did, they started to notice a loud, rumbling noise above their heads. "What is that noise?" Rachel asked, clapping her hands over her ears as it became even louder. "It's awful!"

"It sounds like it's coming from the treehouse," Kirsty said, glancing upward.

Nia nodded. "I think someone's snoring *very* loudly!" she said with a frown. "We'd better fly up there and check it out."

Rachel and Kirsty followed Nia up to the treehouse, passing the owl's nest on the way. The mother had gone to hunt for food, and only the three babies were left, blinking their huge eyes as Nia and

the girls passed
by.

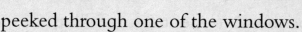

Rachel, Kirsty,
and Nia reached
the treehouse and
peeked through one of the windows.
They could hardly believe what they saw.
Four goblins were inside the treehouse,
curled up in different positions under cozy
blankets. They were all fast asleep and
snoring loudly.

"Perfect!" Kirsty whispered, trying not to laugh. "Now we'll have a chance to search for the magic bag."

"We'll have to be quick," Nia replied in a low voice. "If we don't find it, humans will be the next ones to start falling asleep while it's still daylight!"

Nia and the girls flew through the window into the treehouse. But before they could search for the bag, they heard shrill, squawking sounds behind them.

Whoo! Whoo! WHOO!

Rachel spun around and saw the baby owls calling from their nest, looking scared.

"Oh, no!" Rachel groaned. "The baby owls must be scared of the loud snoring, and they're calling for their mother."

WHOO! the owls squawked.

"And they've woken up the goblins!" Kirsty added in dismay as the goblins began to stir.

They were going to wake up and see the girls any minute!

Topsy-Turvy

Rachel spotted the mother owl flying back through the trees to comfort her babies. But it was too late. The four goblins were already awake, and they sat up yawning and rubbing their eyes. They all looked extremely annoyed!

"It's still daytime," one of them said grumpily. "We're supposed to be asleep!"

At that moment, the smallest goblin spotted Nia, Rachel, and Kirsty hovering by the window.

"I bet *they* woke us up by making silly noises!" the smallest goblin cried. He pointed an accusing finger at them. "Horrible fairies!"

"Ignore them," ordered a long-nosed goblin. "We'll just go and find somewhere else to sleep until the sun sets. It's only a short time from now."

Still complaining loudly, the goblins began tucking their pillows under their arms and rolling up their blankets.

"It's silly sleeping in the daytime," the smallest goblin muttered angrily. "We're *supposed* to go to sleep at night."

"Stop moaning!" snapped one of the other goblins, who had huge ears. "You know Jack Frost is having trouble sleeping, so he wants everyone else's sleep to be mixed up, too."

"And anyway," the long-nosed goblin added, grabbing his pillow, "if we sleep all day, that means we get to stay up and play all night!"

Nia turned to Rachel and Kirsty. "I wonder why Jack Frost is having trouble getting to sleep," she whispered. "Maybe that's why he hates the nighttime so much."

The smallest goblin was still looking very pouty. "Well, *I'm* not sleeping very well, either," he muttered. "You all have nice, cozy blankets, but mine isn't comfy at all!" He shot a jealous glance at the long-nosed goblin's blanket. "I want *that* one!"

"No way!" the long-nosed goblin cried. But the small goblin grabbed a corner of the blanket and tried to pull it out of the other one's arms. The long-nosed goblin wrestled it away from him.

"I'll show you *exactly* how cozy this blanket is!" he yelled. He grabbed the smallest goblin and began rolling him up inside it! The small goblin gave a shriek as he was left rolled up inside the blanket with just his head sticking out of one end and his feet sticking out of the other.

"And *I* got the flattest pillow," the goblin with the big ears grumbled loudly. "It's not fair. Everyone else's is *much* fluffier than mine!" Then he lunged forward, trying to steal the fourth goblin's pillow.

"Stop it!" the fourth goblin squealed, swinging the pillow at him and almost hitting Nia, Rachel, and Kirsty. They fluttered out of the way just in time. Instead, the fourth goblin accidentally hit the

long-nosed goblin right in the face.

"Oh, no you don't! Now I'm *really* angry!" the long-nosed goblin howled. He grabbed his own pillow and began whacking the fourth goblin. Meanwhile, the smallest goblin had unrolled himself and began attacking the big-eared goblin. Soon, a huge pillow fight was underway! Nia and the girls had to keep flying around the treehouse to avoid getting hit.

"I wonder where Nia's bag of sleep dust is." Kirsty gasped as she dodged yet another pillow. "It must be here somewhere."

"Just make sure you don't get hurt, girls," Nia advised as the big-eared goblin hurled his blanket on top of the smallest goblin, trapping him underneath. "The goblins will calm down soon, and then maybe we can find my magic bag."

Rachel nodded. It was then that she saw the long-nosed goblin sneaking over to the door of the treehouse.

The others hadn't noticed that he was creeping away while they kept fighting and arguing. But Rachel could also see that he was holding a ragdoll goblin.

Curious, Rachel flew a little lower. The ragdoll was green, like the goblins, and it was wearing patched overalls with a big

pocket on the front. Rachel almost burst with excitement as she spotted Nia's satin bag poking out of the ragdoll's pocket. "Kirsty!" Rachel called quickly. Her friend was closer to the door and the long-nosed goblin.

"Look at the ragdoll!"

Kirsty immediately glanced down and saw the doll the long-nosed goblin was holding. Her eyes widened and she swooped toward him to grab it. Rachel

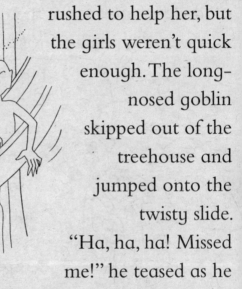

rushed to help her, but the girls weren't quick enough. The long-nosed goblin skipped out of the treehouse and jumped onto the twisty slide. "Ha, ha, ha! Missed me!" he teased as he zoomed down the slide toward the underground fort.

The other goblins rushed after him and followed him down the slide. Nia, Rachel, and Kirsty flew after them, but they couldn't catch up. They were just in time to see the smallest goblin shoot into the underground fort and slam the door shut behind him.

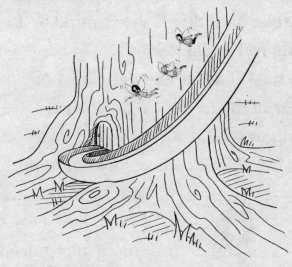

"What are we going to do now?" Rachel panted, feeling very tired all of a sudden. "The bag of sleep dust is hidden in that ragdoll, but we can't get into the underground fort!"

"We'll have to wait until the goblins come out," Nia replied as they fluttered back to the treehouse. "When it's dark, they'll wake up again."

Kirsty yawned widely. "I hope I can stay awake until then!" she remarked. "I suddenly feel really sleepy."

"Me, too." Rachel slumped down on the floor of the treehouse and began yawning as well.

"Oh, no!" Nia frowned, looking from Kirsty to Rachel. "Now Jack Frost's topsy-turvy sleep is affecting humans, just like I thought it would!"

"I'm sorry, Nia," Kirsty murmured, curling up on the floor next to Rachel. "But I'm just so sleepy."

"I can't keep my eyes open," Rachel whispered as she rested her head on her arm.

The last sounds the girls heard were the baby owls chirping in their nest, still wide awake. And just a few seconds later, Rachel and Kirsty were both fast asleep.

Zipline Show!

"Oh!" Rachel opened her eyes and sat up. She blinked, trying to remember where she was. "What's that noise?"

Kirsty sat up, too. "What's happening?" she asked in a dazed voice. Both she and Rachel were now back to their human size.

"You fell asleep, girls." Nia was perched on the window ledge, smiling down at

them. "The sun set while you were asleep, and now that it's dark, you've both woken up again. I made you humans again, just in case anyone came along and found you."

"But what is that noise?" asked Kirsty as they heard shouting and loud, stomping footsteps.

"The goblins are awake, and they're coming out to play!" Nia replied with a frown.

Rachel and Kirsty rushed over to the window and peeked out of the treehouse. The Adventure Playground was now lit up by a pale moon and a sky full of shining silver stars. Below, they could see the goblins rushing out of the underground fort, yelling with delight.

"Yippee!" the smallest goblin shouted

gleefully. "It's nighttime!"

Nia and the girls watched as the long-nosed goblin came out of the underground house behind the others. He was still carrying the ragdoll, but now it was strapped to his chest in a carrier, like a baby.

"Here's the magic sleep dust!" the long-nosed goblin said proudly. He took Nia's bag from the ragdoll's pocket, opened it, and sprinkled a handful of magic sleep dust into the air. It burst around the goblins in a shower of dazzling sparkles.

As Nia and the girls watched, several
gray squirrels suddenly scurried past the
treehouse. They were bright eyed and
wide awake as they leaped
from branch to branch.
"Those squirrels should
be asleep!" Nia
murmured, looking upset.
Meanwhile, Rachel had cocked
her head to one side. Now she was listening
hard.

"I can hear the cows mooing and the
sheep baaing in the distance," she said.
"They should be asleep, too."

"I can hear something else!" Kirsty
pointed in the direction of the campsite.
"It sounds like people talking."

"Yes, people who should be getting
ready for bed by now!" Nia sighed. "Jack

Frost got his wish. Everyone's sleep is all mixed up! Girls, we have to get my bag back somehow, and fast."

"We need a plan," Kirsty said thoughtfully. She stared down at the goblins who were climbing up the ladders to the treetop walkways. "Maybe you should turn us into fairies again, Nia."

But Rachel shook her head. "No, I think I have an idea," she said. "You know how the goblins love to show off?"

Nia and Kirsty nodded.

"Well, maybe Kirsty and I can fool them into thinking we're scared of the Adventure Playground," Rachel explained. "Then, while they're showing off, Nia can fly down

and grab her bag."

"Good idea!" Nia exclaimed.

Rachel and Kirsty hurried out of the treehouse. Nia followed, but remained in the shadows out of sight.

"Be careful," Kirsty called to the goblins. "I almost fell off one of those ladders."

"That's because you're not as strong and brave as we are!" the smallest goblin snapped back, sticking his tongue out at her. He rushed up the ladder and jumped onto the walkway where the girls were standing. Rachel gave a squeal as the walkway shook a little.

"Don't do that!" she exclaimed. "I don't like it."

Grinning, the goblin ran toward them. Making small pretend squeaks of fear, Rachel and Kirsty ran along the walkway toward one of the other trees. But then the big-eared goblin climbed up and blocked their way.

"Oh, no! Rachel!" Kirsty wailed, secretly winking at her friend. "We'll have to cross the wobbly bridge to get away from them."

"But that's really scary!" Rachel complained.

All four of the goblins were laughing now as they chased the girls across the wobbly bridge.

"Go away!" Kirsty shouted.

"Scaredy-cats!" the long-nosed goblin sneered. Rachel noticed that he still had the ragdoll tucked safely inside the carrier on his chest. "Why don't you go on the zipline?"

"Oh, I couldn't do that!" Kirsty gasped in a frightened voice. "The seat zooms so fast."

"I'll show you how to do it!" the long-nosed goblin boasted. He climbed onto one of the ziplines and sat on the seat. "Here goes!"

The goblin set off and flew confidently along the cable toward the opposite tree. As he did, Kirsty saw Nia fly out of the shadows. The fairy swooped down from above the long-nosed goblin and made a grab for the bag in the ragdoll's pocket.

But the goblin spotted Nia immediately.
He screamed with anger and clutched
the ragdoll tightly to his chest with one
hand while holding onto the zipline with
the other. Nia darted forward again and
again, but there was no way she could
pull the bag of magic dust away from the
goblin.

Kirsty and Rachel looked at each other
with disappointment.

"Nia can't get close enough to grab the
bag!" Kirsty said. "What do we do now,
Rachel?"

Shadow
Swoops In

Before Rachel could reply, Shadow the owl suddenly came swooping down from the trees. She rushed toward the goblin. Her magic white-and-silver feathers glittered in the pale moonlight as she flapped her wings and hooted loudly.

The long-nosed goblin looked terrified.

"Leave me alone!" he yelled, trying to shoo Shadow away with one hand and hold onto the zipline *and* the ragdoll with the other.

Rachel saw her chance. She leaped onto the second zipline, which ran next to the one the long-nosed goblin was on, and zoomed off. Rachel was a long way behind the goblin, but Nia spotted her on the zipline and guessed what she was up to. The fairy pointed her wand at the

goblin and a burst of sparkling magic slowed his zipline down.

The goblin didn't notice because he was so focused on fighting off Shadow. He didn't even see Rachel coming toward him! Rachel tensed as she got closer and closer, her eyes fixed on the ragdoll's pocket. Then, as she swept past the goblin, Rachel reached out and grabbed for the bag of magic dust.

But she ended up pulling the whole ragdoll out of the carrier as she zipped by.

"Nice work, Rachel!" Nia called. The goblins, who were waiting below for their friend, had seen what had happened and groaned loudly. Meanwhile, Nia flew over to Rachel and took the magic bag from the ragdoll's pocket.

Still holding the ragdoll, Rachel reached the bottom of the zipline and jumped off. Looking very sheepish, the long-nosed goblin climbed off his zipline, too.

"What's Jack Frost going to say, now that the fairies have the bag of magic sleep dust back?" the smallest goblin yelled at him. "Oh, be quiet!" snapped the long-nosed goblin. "I'll tell him it was all your fault!"

Grumbling and bickering, the goblins trudged off through the trees. The long-nosed goblin was last, dragging his

blanket with him and muttering under

his breath.
Rachel ran
after him and
handed him
the ragdoll.
"Thanks!" the
goblin mumbled,
glaring at her.

Meanwhile, Kirsty had zipped down
the twisty slide from the treehouse to join
Nia, Rachel, and Shadow.

"I can't hear the farm animals
anymore," Kirsty said happily. "And the
camp's quiet now, too. Listen!"

They listened, but all they could hear
were the sounds of the mother owl and
her babies hooting in their nest, and
the rustle of badgers sniffing around

for food in the bushes.

"Everything's back to normal!" Nia exclaimed happily. "Thanks to you, girls—and Shadow, of course! Now I need to rush back to Fairyland. Everyone will be awake now, and I can give them the good news."

Nia waved her wand, and a mist of sparkles shrank Shadow down to her fairy size. Then, calling good-bye, Nia and Shadow flew off to Fairyland, their wings glowing against the dark night sky.

Quickly, Rachel and Kirsty hurried back through the campsite to their tent where everyone was getting ready for bed.

"I really thought we wouldn't be able to get the bag back from the goblin," Rachel whispered. "I'm so glad we did!"

Kirsty nodded. But as they reached their tent, both girls heard a very loud rumbling sound.

"My dad's already gone to sleep—and he's snoring!" Kirsty murmured to Rachel, trying not to laugh. "I wish I had a little of Nia's magic sleep dust to stop him from making so much noise. Then we could *all* have a peaceful night!"

THE NIGHT FAIRIES

Rachel and Kirsty have helped Nia,
and now it's time to help

Anna
the Moonbeam Fairy!

Join their next nighttime adventure
in this special sneak peek. . . .

Mirror, Mirror

It was a cool, dark evening. Kirsty Tate and Rachel Walker were standing with a group of children at the edge of Mirror Lake — a wide, still expanse of water surrounded by hills. The two friends were staying with their families at a vacation spot called Camp Stargaze. They were having a wonderful week so far.

As its name suggested, Camp Stargaze was the perfect place to see the night sky in all its glory, and there were lots of unusual and exciting activities for the campers to do every night. So far, Kirsty and Rachel had been to a campfire midnight feast, gone firefly-watching in the Whispering Woods, and studied the stars from the Camp's observatory. Tonight, they were about to set sail on a moonlit boat ride!

"Come on, you landlubbers," called Peter, the camp counselor. He led them along a small wooden dock, and Kirsty and Rachel saw that a motorboat was tied to the dock. "All aboard, me hearties!"

Chatting and laughing, the children climbed aboard. The boat was lit with lanterns that cast golden reflections onto the dark water of the lake. The boat rocked gently as people took their seats, and Kirsty excitedly squeezed Rachel's hand once they'd sat down. "Every time I go on a boat it reminds me of the first time we met," she said. "Do you remember?"

Rachel smiled at her. The two girls had met on a ferry one summer when their families were both going on vacation to Rainspell Island. Kirsty and Rachel had liked each other immediately, and had ended up having the most amazingly magic time together that week—and they'd shared lots of adventures ever since!

"Of course I remember," Rachel replied. "And I hope—" She broke off as Lucas and Matt, two boys that they'd become friends with, sat down nearby. The girls knew that they couldn't let anyone find out their secret: that they were friends with the fairies — friends who were often called to Fairyland to help on important missions!

Kirsty could guess what Rachel had been about to say — that she hoped they had another fairy adventure that night! "I hope so, too," she whispered quickly. The girls had been helping the Night Fairies search for their stolen bags of magic dust all week, but there were still two bags they hadn't been able to track down.

RAINBOW magic™

There's Magic in Every Series!

The Rainbow Fairies

The Weather Fairies

The Jewel Fairies

The Pet Fairies

The Fun Day Fairies

The Petal Fairies

The Dance Fairies

The Music Fairies

The Sports Fairies

The Party Fairies

The Ocean Fairies

The Night Fairies

Read them all!

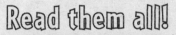

d associated
arks and/or
arks of Scholastic Inc.
Magic Limited
ntertainment logo are
T Entertainment Limited.

www.scholastic.com

www.rainbowmagiconline.com

RMFAIF

RAINBOW magic

These activities are magical!
Play dress-up, send friendship notes, and much more!

and the HIT Entertainment logo are
marks of HIT Entertainment Limited.
2010 Rainbow Magic Limited.
LASTIC and associated logos are trademarks
/or registered trademarks of Scholastic Inc.

■SCHOLASTIC
www.scholastic.com
www.rainbowmagiconline.com